DRAGON STORM

Mira and Flameteller

DRAGON STORM

Mira and Flameteller

ALASTAIR CHISHOLM

nosy crow

First published in the UK in 2022 by Nosy Crow Ltd
The Crow's Nest, 14 Baden Place,
Crosby Row, London SE1 1YW, UK

Nosy Crow Eireann Ltd
44 Orchard Grove, Kenmare,
Co Kerry, V93 FY22, Ireland

Nosy Crow and associated logos are trademarks
and/or registered trademarks of Nosy Crow Ltd

ISBN: 978 1 83994 004 0

A CIP catalogue record for this book is available from the British Library

Printed and bound in Great Britain by Clays Ltd, Elcograf S.p.A.

Papers used by Nosy Crow are made from wood grown in sustainable forests.

1 3 5 7 9 10 8 6 4 2

www.nosycrow.com

IN THE LAND OF DRACONIS, THERE ARE NO DRAGONS.

Once, there were. Once, humans
and dragons were friends, and guarded
the land. They were wise, and strong, and
created the great city of Rivven together.

But then came the Dragon Storm, and
the dragons retreated from the world
of humans. To the men and women of
Draconis, they became legends and myth.

And so, these days, in the land of Draconis,
there are no dragons…

…Or so people thought.

MIRA

"Wake up!" shouted Mira. "Wake up, everyone, it's Wheel Day!"

She went to Erin's bed and shook her shoulder.

"Erin, it's Wheel Day!"

Erin, who had been fast asleep, growled. She peered at Mira with one bleary eye.

"It's *early*," she complained. "And there's no such thing as Wheel Day."

"There is!" shouted Mira happily. "And it's

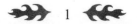

today! Come on!"

She ran to the third bed in their shared dorm hut. "Wake up, Cara!"

Cara was just a lump under her covers. "G'way," the lump muttered.

"But it's *Wheel Day*!" Mira laughed. "I'm going to help Hilda get breakfast ready, so we can set off early!"

"Mmmf," muttered Erin, and rolled over.

It *was* quite early, Mira admitted to herself as she left the dorm. The light was still dim and there was no one around. In the outside world, the sun would just be rising … but not here. Because Mira, the dorm, and everything around her, weren't in the outside world.

Mira and Flameteller

They were in the Dragonseer Guild Hall.

The Hall was a vast cavern, lit up by soft glowing globes that hung above like tiny suns. There were training areas, a racetrack, dormitories, dining huts, classrooms and offices, and more, older buildings off in the distance. It had everything Mira and her friends needed.

Mira closed her eyes, relaxed, and called up the special magic she had been taught on her first day as a dragonseer. She felt a whispering connection…

And the dragon Flameteller appeared.

Flameteller was quite small, just taller than Mira herself, with a stumpy body and a long neck. He was coloured bronze and brown,

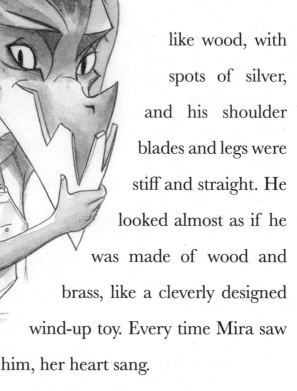

like wood, with spots of silver, and his shoulder blades and legs were stiff and straight. He looked almost as if he was made of wood and brass, like a cleverly designed wind-up toy. Every time Mira saw him, her heart sang.

He stretched his wings with a *click-click-click* sound. "Good morning, Mira!" he chirped. "Is it Wheel Day today?"

Mira grinned. "Yes! But everyone else is being lazy. I'm off to help Hilda with breakfast. Want to come?"

"Of course!"

Flameteller trotted beside her to the dining hut, where they found Hilda preparing breakfast. Hilda was tall and strong-shouldered, always busy, and always had her sleeves rolled up. She smiled at Mira and Flameteller.

"You're up early, my loves!" she said.

"I couldn't sleep," said Mira. "It's Wheel Day! We're off to see the Rivven Wheel!"

Flameteller clicked his wings. "It's the biggest waterwheel in the *world*! It might be the biggest *machine* in the world! Mira's told me all about it."

"We thought we'd come and help with breakfast," said Mira. "Nobody else is awake yet – can you imagine!"

"It's a mystery," said Hilda, smiling. "Well, some help would be lovely. Come on in, but wash your hands and face, Mira – you're covered in grease as usual!"

Mira laughed and washed at the water pump, peering at her reflection in the hut window. Hilda was right. Mira's long black hair was tied into a ponytail with a greasy rag, and the soft brown of her skin was daubed with streaks of black. Mira loved tinkering with machinery, and somehow always came away covered with streaks and marks.

She went into the hut and helped Hilda get breakfast together. Flameteller was too large to fit in the hut, so he stuck his head in the window and they chatted. The other children eventually wandered along, yawning, and Hilda and Mira served them breakfast. Then there was clearing away, and dishes, and finally – finally! – the others started getting ready. Mira was bursting with impatience!

But at last they stood in a semicircle round Lady Berin, Chancellor of the Dragonseer Guild, with their dragons next to them.

Every dragon is different. That was one of the first things Mira had learned when she joined the Dragonseer Guild. She remembered her first day, the first time she saw the Guild Hall.

DRAGON STORM

"The world of dragons is not like ours," Berin had told her. "It is a world of *ideas*. When a dragon first steps into our world, they find their form, and that depends on the dragonseer who summons them. They are your dragon, and you are their human."

And just as every dragon was unique, so was their *power* – the special magic that they, and only they, could do. Some had discovered theirs already. The dragon that Tom, the blacksmith's son, summoned, was Ironskin, a large, powerful beast the colour of flames and hammered iron. She could create a shield to protect others.

Ellis was an explorer, and his stumpy

brown dragon Pathseeker was clever and practical, and could see through illusions. Cunning Cara's dragon Silverthief could turn invisible, for a while. Others were still figuring out their powers – like Flameteller, or Kai and his white and red dragon Boneshadow, or Connor and Lightspirit. Poor Erin was still getting the hang of summoning and needed help to bring her enormous dragon Rockhammer into the human world.

"Is everyone ready for our trip?" asked Berin. Mira and Flameteller nodded vigorously, and the others laughed.

Berin smiled. "Well, Mira, why don't you lead the way?"

Mira grinned and set off towards the doors at the far end of the Hall that led out to the city. As she reached them, Flameteller said, "Time for me to go."

Mira nodded and bumped heads gently with the little dragon, and then Flameteller faded from sight. Around her, the other children smiled and waved to their own dragons as they disappeared.

"Flame?" whispered Mira.

Hello! came Flameteller's voice in her head, and Mira smiled.

They left the Hall and walked along the twisting passageways that led out to the city. These were the Clockwork Corridors, and Mira loved them. They were part of

the defences of the Guild – a maze that
moved under their feet, a clever machine to
fool anyone trying to enter the Dragonseer
Guild. Floor tiles slotted into place around
them, doors and passages opened ahead,
and Mira felt the thrum of machinery under

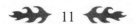

her feet. At last they reached the exit, hidden in a small cottage.

They left the cottage and stepped out into the city of Rivven.

THE RIVVEN
WHEEL

Rivven was the largest city in Draconis, and the oldest. Its streets and houses pushed and piled on top of each other, and narrow lanes squeezed between houses, markets, tanners, merchant halls and smithies. And above them all loomed the mighty Palace Rock, with the gleaming white walls of the Royal palace on top.

Berin marched her students through the bustling streets. Occasionally, rich merchants or city leaders nodded to her, and she nodded back, for out here she was Lady Berin, a city magistrate. Almost no one knew her secret role as head of the Dragonseer Guild. Officially, the children were apprentice clerks, and they wore their brown apprentice cloaks and followed as neatly as they could.

They left through the South Gate, and Berin led them along the road towards the southern hills. She was tall, and walked in brisk long strides, and the children had to trot to keep up.

"This way!" she trilled. "Oh, isn't it nice to breathe some fresh air?"

At the back of the group, Connor groaned. "How much *further*? It's been miles!"

Mira and Flameteller

Connor wasn't much of an outdoor person. His idea of happiness was to be curled up with a book, ignoring everything else.

Erin laughed. "It's been one mile if that, slow-bones!" Erin was tall and athletic, and went running *for fun*. She towered over Mira and positively glowed with health. She and Connor almost never agreed on anything.

Connor muttered something under his breath and staggered on.

"Come on!" Mira called, skipping ahead. "It's just over this hill! Race you!"

Erin grinned and chased after her. Mira reached the top, panting but just ahead, and gazed down into a small valley. From the south came the deep and fast-moving River

Seek, driving between the hills towards Rivven. But halfway along, an ancient stone channel forced the river down to a single point, furious and spitting, until it thundered over a huge, ancient waterwheel.

The Rivven Wheel.

The wheel was vast. Its spokes were huge beams of oak, black and pitted with centuries of use. Its blades were as big as boats, and the huge iron pins that held it in place were wider and longer than Erin. As it turned, it made a *SH-SH-SH* sound, on and on, while above it the river roared and the axle creaked.

"Oh…" Mira gasped. "It's *beautiful.*"

Erin glanced at her.

"It's just a big wheel, Mira."

It IS beautiful! came Flameteller's excited
voice in Mira's mind, and she smiled.
Then Berin started down the hill, and Mira
scurried after her.

Next to the wheel were a collection of

large work buildings, wet from the river and thick with moss, but made of strong, neat bricks. An old man waited outside, dressed in brown boots, a brown coat and a brown shapeless hat. He had wide shoulders and a square jaw, and he was smiling.

"Afternoon, Your Ladyship," he said, removing his hat and bowing.

"Good afternoon, Joshua," said Berin. "Thank you for letting us visit. Students, this is Joshua, and he is our guide. Listen to what he says, and don't touch anything or go anywhere without checking with him. A waterwheel can be very dangerous!"

"Come on in," young' uns he said, and led them inside.

Mira and Flameteller

The waterwheel turned under the force of the water, its pulleys and cogwheels transferring power to other places. There was a mill, grinding wheat into fine flour between two huge stones; a factory crushing rocks from a nearby lead mine; even a mechanical hammer, pounding sheets of iron. Everywhere rang with the sound of industry and the roar of the wheel.

Joshua showed the children around. Tom, whose father was a blacksmith, was interested in the hammer; Kai, who loved animals and nature, looked a bit bored. But Mira stared at everything with her mouth hanging open in wonder. She felt the thrum of the work beneath her feet and heard the whirr of pulleys and the clank of gears, and almost laughed with delight.

"Wonderful!" she gasped.

Erin rolled her eyes. "You're so weird." But she was grinning, and Mira grinned back.

Finally, Joshua led them into a smaller room at the back, which had thick walls that calmed the sound of machinery to a quiet drone. He closed the door behind them and nodded to Berin.

She stepped forward. "Students," she said quietly, "the Dragonseer Guild must stay secret, but we do have friends, here and there." She bowed to Joshua, and he smiled. "And there's something we'd like to show you today."

Mira and Flameteller

Joshua led them over to the hearth. Taking a rag, he rubbed away the brick dust to reveal a mark carved into the stone: three short vertical lines.

"Who can tell me what this means?" asked Berin.

Connor said, "It's dragon, miss. It means it's dragon-made."

Berin smiled. "That's right."

Dragons? asked Flameteller's voice. *We made this?*

Berin faced the group. "You are *dragonseers*. Each of you has the power to allow a dragon into this world. It is a wonderful thing, but these days, a dangerous thing too. We all know what humans think of dragons. We know that many are scared. There are wild stories, and false histories.

"But once, dragons and humans worked together. This waterwheel is an ancient wonder – over a thousand years old – one of the first things built by humans and dragons together. And this is their mark."

The children gazed at the carved lines, until Berin nodded again to Joshua, and he took a handful of dust and rubbed it back over the brickwork.

"Now," she said, "are there any questions?"

Mira's hand shot up.

"What's the maximum capacity at the head-race point?"

Berin blinked. "Er… The what?"

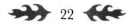

"The point where the water goes on to the wheel," said Mira. "What's the maximum capacity? How do you cope with overflow?"

"Well—"

"Ooh, how much force does it generate? Why does it use a backshot system? Is it for improved efficiency? How often do you have to replace the blades? Is there a reason they're shaped like that? What does—"

Berin raised a hand. "Well, I really meant about the *history* of the building. But if

Joshua doesn't mind, I'm sure he can answer your questions. And since that may take a while −" the others laughed – "we'll eat lunch on the hillside."

They left, leaving just Joshua and Mira.

"Now, miss," said Joshua, smiling. "What would you like to know?"

Mira's eyes gleamed.

"*Everything.*"

Mira chatted non-stop as they walked back to the city. "And the wheel runs backwards to reduce turbulence, see, and the blades are at that angle because it lets them catch the water and release it quickly. Did you know it used to power a rail cart? It pulled it all the way up from Rivven! And—"

"Argh!" shouted Erin. "The only thing more boring than that wheel is you going on about it!"

Mira stopped. "What? But it was *brilliant*! You know, the Guild Hall must use a lot of power. All the moving walkways, and the lights. How does that work? Lady Berin, does the Guild have a waterwheel?"

Ahead of them, Berin shook her head. "No, Mira. We have something else. Perhaps one day you can see."

"Cool!"

It was late afternoon when they reached the city gates again.

"Well, children," said Berin. "I hope you

enjoyed that. Remember – no matter what you hear – there was a world once where dragons and humans were friends. It's our job to make that world again."

But just inside the gates she stopped, and stared up at a huge banner strung between two buildings. Mira looked up too, and her mouth opened in dismay.

"Oh, no," she murmured.

DRAGON SCOURGE

The banner had a picture of a horrible fierce dragon, breathing fire. Next to the dragon was a man in a crown and armour, holding a long spear. He was stabbing the dragon, and the dragon was writhing in agony.

DEATH TO DRAGGUNS read the sign.

Is that supposed to be us? asked Flameteller's voice. Mira nodded.

There was a buzz of activity around them. Posters had been pinned up all around, and

Mira heard shouting up ahead.

Berin's face was grim. "Stay close to me, students," she said. "And remember: if anyone asks, you are apprentice clerks."

They walked towards the King's Plaza, an open square that was sometimes a marketplace, sometimes a festival area. Today there was a stage with red and gold drapes, and a crowd was gathering. To the side sat a black carriage with four beautiful black horses. The carriage had no crest or markings, and its curtains were closed.

A herald stepped on to the stage.

"My lords!" he called in a barrel-chested roar. "My lords, ladies and gentlemen!"

The crowd stopped chattering and

turned. The herald held up a scroll. "I bring a proclamation from His Majesty, King Godfic! He instructs me on this day to tell you—"

"I'll handle this," called a voice, and the herald stopped in surprise. Mira realised the carriage door had opened and a hooded figure now stood next to it. The figure leaped lightly on to the stage, patted the startled herald on the back and lifted his hood.

It was Prince Harald, the king's son. The crowd gasped, and many of them kneeled, but he waved them back to their feet.

"No, no," he said. "Thank you, but I am not your king. Please, stand."

Prince Harald was rather handsome, Mira

thought. He had shoulder-length blond hair and a friendly face, and wore a red outfit decorated with silver thread patterns. He smiled as the people stood again.

"As you know," he said, "my father counts the safety of Rivven and the land of Draconis above all things, and protects us from evil. But there are rumours of a danger from our past, come to haunt us again."

His voice was serious, and as he looked around the people stayed hushed.

"I am talking about dragons," he said.

Mira gasped. Beside her, Berin pursed her lips but gave no other expression. The crowd murmured.

"We had not wanted to believe it," said the prince. "But recently an item under royal protection was stolen from the king's own chambers. It was a tool of old magic. Old *dragon magic*. And it can only be used by those who are in league with dragons."

There was a burst of excited chatter, but Prince Harald spoke over it.

"There are those who have chosen to

side with dragons, against their own kind!" he roared. "Pretending to be your friends, but secretly bringing back these terrible creatures! Here in Rivven – perhaps in this very square!"

Everyone in the crowd looked around, peering into each other's faces, searching for guilt. Berin's face stayed calm, and she gazed at the prince as if mildly interested in a curious idea. Mira and the others tried to copy her. The city, normally so friendly and bustling, suddenly felt very hostile.

"My father, King Godfic, Dragon Scourge, is sworn to protect Draconis," continued Prince Harald. "And he has ordered me to root out these traitors! We will search every building in this city, and we will not stop until we have found them *and* their terrible creatures … and *destroyed* them! Who's with me?"

The crowd *roared* with a mix of anger and delight. They cheered, thumped each other on the backs, and some of them even started waving their daggers and swords in the air.

Berin sighed. "This is no place for children," she said primly. "Come along."

She led them away from the square.

"That's all *lies*!" snapped Erin. "Why would he say that?"

"Quiet now," murmured Berin. "We'll discuss it later."

I don't like this, said Flameteller's voice in

her mind. He sounded worried. *The humans are scared of us. Scared humans do strange things.*

They passed the black carriage, and Mira saw another man standing there, dressed in the traditional black cloak of a clerk. It was Malik. Malik lived in the palace as the king's clerk. He was also, secretly, a member of the Dragonseer Guild and often brought them warnings or information. Now his face was pale and shocked, but he tried to smile as he saw them.

"Clerk Malik," said Berin formally.

"Lady Berin," he said, bowing. "You are back from your trip, I see. Did my young apprentices enjoy their history lesson?"

"I think we are learning all sorts of things

today," said Berin.

Malik nodded. "I will be in touch, my lady, to discuss their timetables. It might be a good time to take a short holiday…"

Berin smiled. "Perhaps. Good day, Malik."

He bowed again, and she led the children away.

"They must be talking about the Dragon's Eye," Tom said to Ellis as they walked. The Dragon's Eye was a magical jewel that Ellis had seen during the Maze Festival the previous month.

Ellis nodded. "Yes. But it was the princess who took it, not us!"

"Maybe someone should tell the king,"

suggested Connor.

"No," said Berin. "We cannot place the princess in that situation. Besides…" She sighed. "This isn't about the Eye. King Godfic is determined to wipe out dragons and the Eye is just his latest excuse. He wants to whip the crowd up into fear and use that."

"And Prince Harald?" asked Mira.

Berin shrugged. "As prince, he must follow his father's orders. Here we are."

She led the children into a narrow side alley towards the tiny, broken-down cottage that hid the Guild Hall entrance. Carefully checking around, they entered the cottage and approached a plain cupboard door. Mira felt a faint whirr beneath her feet, and

then a *click*, and the passageway opened.
The door clicked shut behind them, and
the corridor moved.

But this time Mira was too worried to
think about the machinery, and even
the corridors seemed to feel it;
they stuttered and bumped
as they moved. Berin
frowned as she waited
for the last corridor to
lurch into position.

They reached the
large   doorway
at the end of
the passages,
and   Berin

raised her staff. Blue light shimmered, the door opened, and they returned to the Hall.

Mira felt a tremble in the air beside her, and the brown-bronze shape of Flameteller appeared. He nuzzled his head against her shoulder, his skin smooth like polished wood.

"It's all right," he said softly. "And the wheel was fun, wasn't it?"

"Mmm," said Mira. She forced a smile, but she was worried.

THE SEIGE

Being back in the Guild Hall and seeing Flameteller made Mira feel better, and soon they were chattering away.

"Don't worry," she said. "Prince Harald's mob won't get anywhere near you. We'll build a machine to stop them or something. Something enormous!"

Flameteller laughed. There was more laughing over dinner in the children's shared dining hut. Hilda had made spicy stew and dumplings and they tucked in, joking and jostling with each other, and stopped worrying about everything going on outside. Later, Berin summoned them to the training ground. She looked serious, but not worried. Beside her were Daisy, who taught self-defence, and Creedy, the grim and scowling Vice Chancellor.

When everyone was there, Berin smiled.

"Students," she said, "you may be worried about the scene we saw outside. There is fear out there, and sometimes that can spread."

Mira remembered Flameteller's words. *Scared humans do strange things.*

"These things will pass," said Berin. "I believe that people, on the whole, are good, and eventually we *will* persuade them. But for now, we'll lie low. We'll stay here, safe in the Guild Hall, continue our training, and step out again when things have calmed down."

"But what if they find the entrance?" asked Ellis. "Prince Harald said he was going to search every building."

Berin smiled. "The Clockwork Corridors will protect us, as ever. Whenever he or his men come close, we can simply move the passages away."

"What if he finds us anyway?" asked Erin. "Will there be a fight?" She sounded quite keen. By now someone had helped her summon her gigantic dragon Rockhammer, and he bristled his enormous spiky back.

"Let me at 'em," he growled.

Berin raised a hand. "There won't be a fight. This Hall —" she waved up at it — "is just a place, and we can always find another place. You all know about the Dragon Storm, the great war. Humans fought against humans, dragons against dragons. And afterwards the dragons were so appalled they left us for hundreds of years. I won't let that happen again." She shook her head. "No. If Prince Harald were to discover us, the dragons will return to their own world and we will return to ours. The Hall and all of its history may be lost … but we will survive."

"But there's only one way in and out," said Connor.

Berin smiled "There is another way. There is a part of these caves you have not seen yet, and I will show you."

The children murmured. Ellis, who loved exploring and map-making, muttered excitedly to his dragon Pathseeker. Only Erin seemed disappointed there wouldn't be a battle.

"Follow me!" called Berin, and she marched past the group and towards a cluster of storerooms. Inside, the rooms were piled with sacks and barrels, shelves reaching high with equipment and tools – everything needed to keep the Dragonseer Guild running. Berin walked to a half-hidden door at the back and into another room, with a large square hole in the floor and a staircase leading down. Mira heard water lapping against stone and felt a cool breeze against her face, and as she reached the bottom of the stairs she realised they were on a small dock, beside an underground canal.

Ellis gasped in surprise. "I never knew *this* was here!"

Mira peered around. There were coils of rope, and pulleys, and she felt the rumble of machinery. The sides of the canal were built of solid stone slabs, like the waterwheel building. On the far side the slabs stretched up to form a huge wall, and she thought she heard rushing water.

"I think that's the River Seek on the other side of that wall," muttered Ellis, scribbling notes. "This canal must come off it and then rejoin."

A boat came towards them out of the dark, pulled by a rope on a turning wheel.

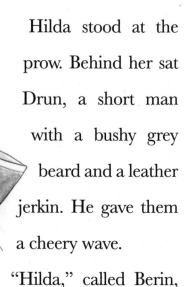

Hilda stood at the prow. Behind her sat Drun, a short man with a bushy grey beard and a leather jerkin. He gave them a cheery wave.

"Hilda," called Berin, "I've brought you and Drun some assistants."

Hilda grinned. "Good timing! We have some supplies to unload!"

The boat was pulled in, and Hilda stepped out and tied it to a post.

"This is how we bring in everything we need to keep the Guild running," said Berin.

"Hilda runs this area, and we all take turns helping." She smiled. "And for a while you'll help too."

"This is the real heart o' the Guild!" said Drun. He chuckled. "Or at least the belly, eh?"

"So you see," said Berin, "we have all we need. And even if Prince Harald somehow found the entrance above, we have a way out. We'll be quite safe. Now! We have supplies to store, and you can all help."

Hilda and Drun unloaded barrels, sacks, legs of salted ham, bags of pepper and other spices, and casks of good fresh water. The children and dragons carried them to a pallet, and some mysterious machinery from above heaved them up to the supply room.

Mira and Flameteller watched it curiously.

"Where *does* all the power come from?" Mira asked.

Berin's eyes twinkled. "Would you like to find out?" she asked.

"What? Yes!"

"Good! Because I have a special job for you. Come with me."

She led Mira away from the dock, to an area blocked by a large wall with a small, heavy door.

"You wanted to know how we power the Guild?" said Berin. "It's through here." She opened the door and entered, and Mira and Flameteller followed her – and their mouths fell open in wonder.

GRIMBAL

Berin, Mira and Flameteller were in a machinery room, like the heart of the Rivven Wheel, but many times larger and busier! Pulleys squealed, wheels spun, gears crashed and meshed, pistons clattered. Above her, conveyer belts trundled and clanged. The whole room seemed to tremble with energy.

"Oh, *wow*!" Mira cried.

"This is *amazing*!" said Flameteller. His eyes glittered as he watched. Mira gazed up at the machinery around her, and for a moment it felt like she was back in her father's workshop.

Mira's father was a clockmaker and always had dozens of clocks ticking, whirring and chiming around him. For as far back as she could remember, Mira had loved to sit on his lap as he showed her his latest mechanical creations, and would look up at the clocks and feel that she could never be happier.

But one day, when she was in the workshop by herself, daydreaming and listening to the machinery, she'd heard something new – a mysterious, half-ticking, half-purring, half-mechanical, half-alive sound. And in among the mess of clock faces and workings she'd seen two small lights, almost like eyes, seeming to gaze back at her.

That had been six months ago, before Malik the king's clerk had unexpectedly visited and offered to make Mira an apprentice clerk. She hadn't been sure she wanted to leave, until he'd secretly explained the truth – that Mira was a *dragonseer*, someone who could reach into the world of dragons and connect to them. She'd met Drun, who had helped her learn how to summon. And then she'd seen Flameteller, rising out of the fire of Drun's hut, with his gorgeous brown and bronze colouring and his strange way of moving, almost like clockwork. A creature of magic, shaped by his link to Mira and her love of all mechanical things. And every day since had felt more extraordinary than the last.

She wished she could show her father Flameteller and tell him about all the things she'd seen. Perhaps one day she could bring him to this incredible room! But for now, she looked at Flameteller's delighted face instead and laughed, and he laughed back.

"Amazing!" he said again.

"This way!" said Berin.

At the end of the room was another door. A hand-painted sign in yellow and black read:

ENGINE ROOM
DO NOT ENTER

Mira and Flameteller

Berin led them through.

There was a workbench and some shelves, a chair, and a few large metal levers in the corner. But the first thing Mira noticed was an enormous wheel, made of brass and iron, mounted flat against the far wall. The wheel turned around the middle, which stayed fixed. There was a design forged on to the front, the same three short lines as at the waterwheel – the sign of something dragon-made.

Mira gazed at it. The wheel turned slowly, but somehow with mighty power. The metal seemed to *thrum* with energy, like a huge coiled spring, or a wild animal. Cautiously, she reached towards it—

"Don't touch that!"

Mira snatched her hand back and whirled. Behind them was a man in a tatty brown coat and boots. He had grey hair, neatly combed, and his face was pulled down into a scowl. He looked like he scowled a lot. His forehead was one big angry wrinkle.

"That's a powerful and delicate device. Leave it alone!"

"Sorry!" squeaked Mira. I was just—"

"You could have been hurt!" the man snapped. "Or even worse – you could have *damaged* it! What are you doing here?"

"I brought them," said Berin gently. "Hello, Grimbal."

The man seemed to notice Berin for the first time, and stopped.

"Yer Ladyship," he said in a grudging voice. "What can I do for you?"

"I'd like to introduce you," said Berin. "Mira, Flameteller, this is Grimbal. You asked how the Guild Hall works. Where the power comes from; how the Clockwork

Corridors move. The answer is Grimbal. He is the genius who keeps everything going."

Grimbal's face softened slightly, although he still looked suspicious.

"And these," said Berin, "are Mira and Flameteller, both promising engineers themselves."

"Hello!" said Mira.

"Hmmph," muttered Grimbal.

"I thought they could assist you for a while," said Berin.

Grimbal blinked. "I don't need an assistant," he said, looking outraged. "I got everything going just right!"

"Of course," said Berin smoothly. "Only ... there are some problems with the Corridors,

I think? Sticking sometimes?"

"Oh," said Grimbal, waving a hand. "I just got to get into the mechanism there—"

"And the lights have been flickering recently," said Berin.

"Well, you know, the lights is old, sometimes they—"

"And I have wondered if the fans have been sometimes spinning loose?"

"Well, I can't do everything!" he protested. "I got a million jobs you don't even *know* about. I got to keep this place going, I got to repair it, I got—"

Berin raised her hands. "Absolutely, Grimbal. I understand you're very overworked. And so I've brought you two assistants."

"But—" Grimbal stopped. He opened his mouth once or twice, and then closed it into a new scowl. "Yes, Yer Ladyship."

"Good!" Berin gave her widest smile. "Mira, Flameteller: Grimbal here is the best engineer I've ever met. He will teach you how all of this works, but you must do what he says, and *only* what he says. Understand?"

Mira and Flameteller glanced at each other. Grimbal still looked very cross.

But the workshop … and this room … and the brass wheel…!

"Yes," said Flameteller.

"*Absolutely*," said Mira.

"Good!" said Berin. "Well then, I'll leave you to it. Good luck!"

She left, leaving Mira, Flameteller and Grimbal looking awkwardly at each other. Eventually, Grimbal sighed.

"Well, you'll need some proper overalls," he said at last. "Come on."

THE DRAGON'S HEART

Grimbal found some old overalls in a back cupboard. They were far too large for Mira, but he picked the smallest set and rolled up the arms and legs.

"Right," he said. "Let's get to work."

Mira was very excited. "So is *everything* powered from here?"

"Yep."

"Even the Clockwork Corridors? The lights? Everything?"

"Yep."

"So where does the power come from?" asked Flameteller. "Is it from that big wheel? What *is* that?"

Grimbal sighed. "S'pose I'd better show you. But no touching, right?"

He opened a brass panel next to the wheel. Inside was a dial with three raised lines, like the dragon mark they'd seen at the Rivven Wheel. Grimbal picked up a tool like a spanner, with a head that fitted over the lines, and heaved at it. The dial turned, and a line formed down the fixed centre of the wheel. And suddenly Mira could see that the centre was in two halves, so neatly fitted together that they seemed like one. They pulled apart…

Inside, something *glowed*.

It shone like a diamond in sunlight, but as if the light was coming from inside it. It was crystal, with flat sides and sharp lines, but it throbbed like a living thing. It pulsed bright and soft, bright and soft.

"Oh…" Mira gasped.

Grimbal nodded. "There are pieces of magic in this world," he said. "No one's sure where they come from, but folk say they're f r a g m e n t s of the dragon realms. There are Dragon's Eyes, that let you see hidden things—"

"Oh, we know about them!" said Mira in a rush. "Ellis and Pathseeker found a girl who—"

Grimbal looked cross. Mira realised she'd interrupted his speech. "Sorry."

He cleared his throat. "*As I was saying*, there are Dragon's Eyes, that let you see hidden things. And there's Dragon's Blood, which they say can give you strength, and Dragon's Breath, rarest of all... Well, this is the Dragon's Heart. Everything here – the Clockwork Corridors, the fans that give us fresh air, the barge pulley, even the lights – they're all powered from this."

"Like a waterwheel," murmured Flameteller. "The Heart turns the wheel, and the wheel turns everything."

Grimbal gave a thin smile. "There ain't a waterwheel in the world as powerful as the Dragon's Heart," he said proudly.

Mira gazed at it. "And you *built* this?"

"What? Oh, goodness, no. Look at the mark!" He pointed to the pattern of three lines. "No, this was dragon-made. Over a thousand years ago, longer even. No. I keep her going, though. Look after her."

The light wasn't completely even. One patch seemed darker, about the size of Mira's hand.

"What's that dark patch?" she asked.

Grimbal sniffed. "Nothing." He closed the sliding panels with a *clang*.

Mira frowned. "It looked like there was something—"

"It's *nothing*," he snapped. "This old thing's been runnin' for over a thousand years. After the Dragon Storm, she was all by *herself*, without anyone to look after her, till we found her again. You try working a thousand years; you'll have a bit o' wear and tear yourself!"

"Sorry," said Mira hurriedly. "I didn't mean—"

"Kids these days," muttered Grimbal. "They come in wet behind the ears and suddenly they're tellin' you how to do your job!"

Mira and Flameteller glanced at each other's ears, but they seemed dry.

"Sorry?" tried Mira.

"Hmmph," he muttered again. "Right. Well, let's get to work."

Mira brightened. "What should we do first? The Corridors? They were sticking when we came in. Or maybe the lights? Or should we—"

"That bench," said Grimbal firmly.

Mira looked at the wooden bench, piled high with old machine parts, ropes, cans and tools.

"You can start by tidying it up."

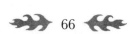

Mira and Flameteller

The rest of the day was incredible!

And frustrating.

And amazing!

And boring.

The engine room powered the whole Guild Hall – every single light and mechanical device within it. The Dragon's Heart's slow but incredibly powerful turns drove huge gear wheels, which turned smaller ones, which pulled conveyor belts and spun crankshafts and moved walkways and carried lifts and heaved ropes and, oh, it was the most *amazing* thing Mira and Flameteller had ever seen!

But they hardly got a chance to see it, because they were tidying the bench.

When they'd finished, Grimbal showed

them the Clockwork Corridors control room, where mighty springs and levers shifted the maze that protected the Guild Hall from hunters!

He handed Mira a broom and told her to sweep up.

Then he repaired one of the globes, that

somehow took the mechanical energy from the Dragon's Heart and turned it into light!

Flameteller held the tools.

"There's all this stuff!" Mira complained later during dinner. "And it all needs repairing, and we could help, but all we're doing is … is *sweeping*!"

Erin shrugged. She crammed an entire bread roll into her mouth.

"You've just started, though," she said in a muffled voice.

"But Grimbal won't let us help! He doesn't even *like* us! Oh, Erin, you should have seen it!"

"We were too busy heaving barrels all

afternoon," said Erin, swallowing.

"Oh." Mira realised she hadn't asked. "Sorry, that was probably much more boring."

Erin chuckled. "Actually, I quite enjoyed it. I can lift a barrel all by myself, did you know that?" She raised an arm and flexed her muscles. "Connor tried, but he couldn't manage." At the end of the table, Connor bristled.

"Well, *some* of us are smart enough to roll them, aren't we?" he snapped. "Instead of showing off!"

"You *tried* to lift it. I saw you!" said Erin, laughing, and the two of them started bickering.

Mira and Flameteller

Mira left them to it. Erin and Connor always found a reason to argue, and sometimes it was fun, but she was too tired to join in. She wandered back to their dorm hut and climbed on to the roof, to the spot where the children sometimes liked to sit. Then she cleared her mind and summoned Flameteller. There was a soft *thump* as the dragon appeared and settled down next to her.

"Oh, Flame," she murmured. "Wasn't it exciting!"

"Did you see the big cogwheels turn?!" exclaimed the dragon.

Mira leaned against the dragon's warm side and gazed up at the lights as they talked about the workshop, and the wheel, and Grimbal. It was settling down to evening now, and the globes above her had dimmed, like stars. But, as she watched, one seemed to stutter. It went dark, and then came back.

Mira frowned. "Did you think there was something odd about the Dragon's Heart?" she asked.

Flameteller nodded. "I could hear it, I think," he said. "It was like a note out of tune."

"Grimbal seemed angry I even asked."

"Perhaps once we've shown him what good engineers we are, he'll trust us a bit more. It was only the first day."

"Yeah." Mira suddenly gave a wide yawn.

Mira and Flameteller

"G'night, Flame."

"Goodnight, Mira."

Mira dragged herself to her feet and Flameteller faded away. He was still around; Mira could feel him in the back of her mind, half in the human world and half out. She smiled, clambered down and got into bed.

How's Eliza doing? asked Flameteller's voice, in her head.

Mira smiled and lifted her lantern to a spot beside her bed. There was a tiny spider there, sitting at the edge of a web that spread several centimetres wide. Mira and Flameteller had watched her build it. Mira loved the way her web grew, and how perfectly she laid each strand, balanced each tension point, a miniature marvel of engineering.

"Night-night, Eliza," murmured Mira. She doused the lamp and settled down. "Night-night, Flame,"

Night-night, Mira, murmured Flameteller's voice, and Mira drifted to sleep.

FIXING

Berin, Creedy and the other adults prepared for a possible siege by Prince Harald, and the young dragonseers and their dragons helped. The Clockwork Corridors were closed now, and the only news they had came from Hilda, as she brought more supplies through the hidden canal.

On the second day, Berin called everyone together again. She looked serious.

"Prince Harald is doing what he promised,"

she said. "He's organised a group to search the city, building by building, looking for the Guild Hall."

Mira and the others gulped.

"Will he find us?" asked Tom.

"No," said Berin. "We'll keep the Corridors closed from now on, so there will be no way to get in. The underground canal comes out at a point far from the centre, where no one will find it. We'll just wait until they get tired of searching."

"How will we know?" asked Cara. "If we can't get in or out?"

Berin nodded. "Vice Chancellor?"

Vice Chancellor Creedy stepped forward. Creedy was a dour, grumpy man, and was usually scowling, or making sharp comments about the children's dragon-riding skills. He was dragging a metal stand, and behind him came Daisy, the combat instructor, bouncy and jolly in green leggings so bright they almost glowed. She carried a silver bowl of water. Creedy positioned the stand and Daisy placed the bowl on top.

"You will all be quiet," he announced in a harsh voice. Berin's lips twitched as if hiding a smile. He ignored everyone and bowed his head. After a few seconds, his dragon appeared.

Creedy's dragon was called Nightwatcher. She was large and completely black, so black that it was hard to make out her features.

Looking at her was like staring into a bottomless pit. Even her teeth and tongue were black. The only colour was in her eyes, which were bright red and sinister. The children took a half-step back.

Nightwatcher stretched her neck and peered into the silver bowl, closed her red eyes and breathed gently on to the water. It rippled and glowed. And then, against the back wall of the Guild Hall cavern, an image appeared.

It shimmered like a reflection, and at first it was too blurry to make out. Creedy rested one hand on Nightwatcher's neck and she shifted. The picture focused.

"It's the city," murmured Ellis.

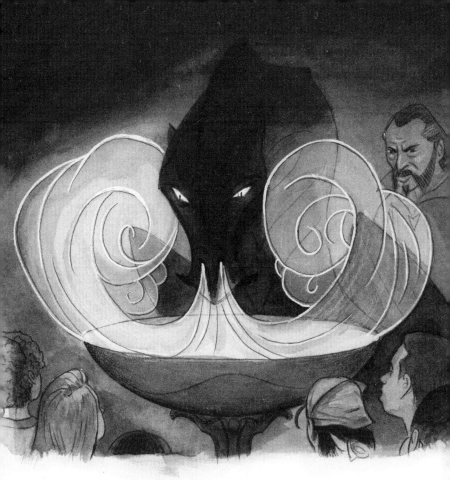

He was right. It was like seeing the city from a great height. Sunlight shone down, and Mira realised she could even see tiny figures moving around.

"Oh!" she said. "It's like a camera

obscura!"

"What's that?" asked Tom.

"A way of projecting an image," said Connor.

"It's really clever," said Mira. "You need a very small aperture, and light comes in and gets projected against a—"

"*Quiet!*" hissed Creedy. He glared a beady eye at Mira.

"Sorry," muttered Mira.

Creedy and Nightwatcher concentrated, and the image moved, like a bird flying over Rivven. It swooped down to a market square and there was Prince Harald, talking to a group of men and women. They looked angry. There was no sound, but he was clearly sending them throughout the city.

"There," said Berin. "We can see where they are, and we're perfectly safe."

She smiled again, reassuringly. The image faded away and Berin dismissed the children. But as they turned away, Mira noticed Berin glancing up at the light globes. One globe was flickering softly.

Later, Berin came to visit them in the engine room.

"Do you know what the problem is?" she asked.

Grimbal looked harassed. "Not *absolutely*, Yer Ladyship," he muttered. "Got some ideas; I'm working through them. Takes time to investigate something like this, y'know."

Berin nodded. "Of course. How can we help?"

Grimbal shook his head. "Oh, I'm on top of it – don't you worry. Soon have it sorted. Yes, yes."

"Maybe it's the Dragon's Heart," said Mira. "Maybe it's to do with that mark."

Berin looked at her sharply. "What?"

Grimbal rolled his eyes. "It ain't that. I've been checking – the Heart's fine. No, it's something in the workings; just got to nail it down." He waved a hand airily. "Girl's new – she doesn't know anything about anything yet."

"Hmm." Berin frowned. "Well, if you're *sure*…"

Mira and Flameteller

"Absolutely." Grimbal beamed. "Got an idea what it might be already. Sort it by tomorrow, for sure."

He waited until Berin had left. Then he turned to Mira and Flameteller.

"Don't you go putting bad ideas on Her Ladyship!" he snapped. "I been working this place since we found it – you think I don't know what's what?"

Mira was shocked. "No! I just thought we should consider all the—"

"You tellin' me I don't know my job?"

"No, I—"

"Get back to work!"

Mira stared at Grimbal. He seemed furious, but there was something else, she thought. Almost … *scared*. He stormed out of the room, and Mira sighed and picked up her broom. The Dragon's Heart continued its steady, huge ticking.

"What was that about?" she asked Flameteller.

"I don't know," said the dragon. "But there *is* something wrong, I can feel it."

"I know! The way Grimbal's acting, it's like—"

"No," interrupted the dragon. He sniffed the air, as if picking up a scent. "I mean, in here. Something… Can you hear it?"

"Hear what?" asked Mira. "It's pretty loud."

Flameteller shook his head. "All of this is

like a song to me," he said, waving a claw up towards the mechanisms above their heads. "Like music. But there's a wrong note somewhere. It's in the wrong place, or the wrong rhythm…" He frowned. "I think it's coming from the Heart."

There was a clatter of metal as Grimbal returned with an armful of parts.

"Here," he said, dropping them on the floor. "Sort this lot out and no lip!"

"Yes, *sir*," muttered Mira.

When he left again, Mira whispered, "We should take a look."

"We can't," replied Flameteller. "Grimbal's here all day."

"Then we should take a look at *night*."

Flameteller hesitated, and then nodded. They got to work.

That evening, Mira and Flameteller sat on the hut roof, waiting for everyone to go to sleep. More of the globes were flickering, Mira thought. And every so often a faint tremble ran through the cavern, as the fans stuttered. At midnight, they sneaked down to the dock. Mira listened to the machinery, and the lapping water of the canal, and the rush of the River Seek on the other side of the river wall, mighty and constant. There was nothing else.

They crept into the engine room and gazed at the great wheel.

Mira and Flameteller

"The bad note is coming from inside," said Flameteller. "There's something wrong with the Heart, but I can't tell what it is."

"We could take a quick peek?" asked Mira. She found the tool Grimbal had used before and turned the dial that opened the cover. It was hard work and Flameteller had to lean on it with her. The metal screeched.

"It didn't do this before," whispered Mira. "I think the cover's swollen."

Finally it opened and the glowing Dragon's Heart appeared.

Flameteller gazed at the dark stain. "It's definitely wrong. Can't you hear it?"

Mira listened. She tried to block out the sounds of machinery. Yes … there was a faint whine. Actually, it was quite clear now. In fact, it seemed to be getting louder.

It was definitely getting louder.

"I think …" she said slowly, "we should close the cover again."

The Heart's light had changed. It was brighter, she thought, but flickering. And the tick of its wheel seemed to be speeding up.

"I can almost hear what it's saying," muttered Flameteller. "Nearly…"

Mira felt a sudden pang of alarm. "Close it," she said. "Close it now, Flame. Something's wrong. Close it!"

Mira and Flameteller

Flameteller blinked in surprise and then nodded. "Yes."

Mira lifted the spanner again. "Ready?"

Suddenly there was a *crash* behind them.

"What are you *doing*?" cried Grimbal. He was bare-footed, wearing an old dressing gown and a nightcap.

"Sorry!" blurted Mira. "We're just looking—"

"Get away from her!" he roared, and rushed towards them.

"We're trying to close it!"

"Away! Leave her alone!" He lunged at Mira, and she shrank back. The spanner was still in her hand.

"Stop!"

They collided, and the spanner swung
back, and hit the Dragon's Heart...
And the Heart screamed.

DISASTER

"Argh!" shouted Mira, clapping her hands over her ears. The Dragon's Heart's scream was a metallic wail that was horrible to hear.

Grimbal stared in horror at the diamond face. "What have you done?" he gasped.

"Nothing!" protested Mira. "We were just looking!"

Beams of light pulsed from the Heart. Flameteller said urgently, "We have to get

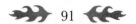

out of here."

"No!" cried Grimbal. "We've got to close the cover!" He grabbed the spanner and tried to turn the dial, but it wouldn't move. The wailing was louder. "Come on!" he hissed. "Close!"

The noise was reaching a shriek, the light pulsing faster than ever. Mira staggered away, dizzy.

"Get away from there!" shouted Flameteller. Grimbal ignored him. Flameteller leaped forward and knocked him to the ground, and Grimbal turned in fury.

"You fool!" he shouted. "I got to—"

A beam of white-blue energy burst from the

Dragon's Heart. It crackled with lightning and roared through the air where Grimbal had been standing, crashing right through the far wall. The bench exploded and bricks and dust flew.

Mira stared through the hole and across the canal, where the lightning had smashed into the ancient river wall. The stone slabs splintered under the pressure, mortar and dust flying everywhere, and the

Dragon's Heart shrieked once more. Then the light stuttered and went out and the Heart dimmed.

"Oh…" moaned Grimbal.

Mira breathed out slowly in the silence.

There was a sound like a *pop*, and a thin jet of water hissed out from between two battered slabs in the river wall. Mira watched it in horrified fascination. *Hissssssssss…*

"Oh, no," she murmured.

And then the river burst through.

A thousand gallons of white frothing water crashed through the wall, carving a hole. On the other side was the River Seek, and it was coming in like the most powerful waterfall Mira had ever seen. It poured down into

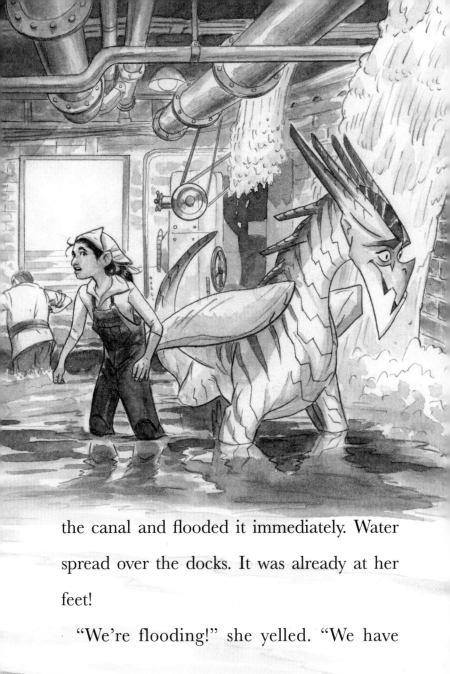

the canal and flooded it immediately. Water

spread over the docks. It was already at her

feet!

"We're flooding!" she yelled. "We have

to go!"

Grimbal scrambled to his feet. "Oh, no!" he wailed. "Oh, no!"

He ran towards a wooden box built into the wall and ripped off the cover. Inside was a long metal lever with a red handle. Grimbal heaved at it.

"Help me!" he roared.

Mira and Flameteller heaved at the lever with him, and at last it moved. Above them, huge weights dropped, and then from the near side of the canal a tall metal barricade slid up – a flood barrier, Mira realised. The canal filled up almost to the top of the barricade, a ferocious torrent of water, far too dangerous to enter.

Mira and Flameteller

Behind them, the Dragon's Heart ticked again, faster than ever, and the wheel round it spun, and now a new sound rang out above them. It was deep, but huge, like a mechanical giant turning over in its sleep, and when Grimbal heard it he gasped.

"The Clockwork Corridors…" he muttered. "They're out of control. They've opened!" The wheel spun madly, screaming, faster and faster—

And stopped.

Everything stopped. All the machinery stopped. The pulleys, crankshafts, conveyer belts, winding ropes, the fans … stopped.

Above them, the dock globe lights faded and the world went dark.

Dragon Storm,

"Oh, girl," whispered Grimbal's voice in the darkness. "What have you *done*?"

Grimbal found a lamp and they waded through the flooded dock and up to the surface. As they left the storerooms, Mira heard worried voices and shouts, and saw little points of light ahead – people carrying lamps, rushing towards them. Berin reached them first. Lamplight swung shadows across her face.

"What happened?" she demanded.

Grimbal gaped at her. "They broke the Dragon's Heart!" he spat. "They *broke* it!"

Mira gasped. "I didn't mean to!" she squeaked. "It was *you*, you made me—"

"What about the Corridors?" asked Berin sharply. "Are they still working?"

Grimbal was almost in tears. "*Nothing's* working," he gasped. "The Corridors are *open!*"

The others had caught up now, adults and children. Beside Berin, Creedy cursed. "If the passage is open, Prince Harald's men can find us," he muttered. "We must evacuate."

"We *can't*," wailed Grimbal. "She broke the river wall too; the canal's impassable!"

Berin's face stayed calm. "Drun," she called into the darkness, "make sure we have lamps for everyone, and lamp oil. Vice Chancellor, call up the scrying glass. I want to know where Prince Harald's mob is at all times. Daisy, prepare our defences." Behind her, the adults scurried away to their tasks. Berin turned back. "Hilda, you and I will go with Mr Grimbal to survey the damage."

"Yes, ma'am," said Hilda.

Grimbal nodded, and they set off.

"Wait!" called Mira. "What can we do?"

"Get some rest," said Berin. She turned to the children and raised her lamp. "All of you, go back to bed. Nothing will happen until the morning."

"But we can help!" said Mira. "We can—"

"*Enough!*" snapped Berin. She shook her head and sighed. "Just ... go away, you two. We'll discuss your actions later."

The adults left. Mira realised the other

children were looking at her.

"Mira, what did you do?" asked Connor.

For a moment, Mira stared at him with her mouth open. Then she burst into tears.

RECOVERY

"And then suddenly there was this beam of – of *energy* or something," sobbed Mira. "And the river wall burst, and Grimbal was shouting…"

She sat on her bed with the others round her. Erin held her hand.

Connor shook his head. "This is really bad," he said. "We can't close the Corridors. We can't use the canal to escape. Without the fans, we might not even have enough fresh air. What were you thinking?"

"Enough," said Kai gently. He put a hand on Connor's shoulder. "Mira already feels bad; you don't need to rub it in."

Connor pursed his lips but didn't answer. It was late, and eventually the boys returned to their dorm.

"Things will seem better in the morning," said Kai as he left, smiling at Mira.

Erin and Cara crept into their bunks. Mira sat by the light of a dim lamp, staring at the wall.

It wasn't our fault, said Flameteller's voice. *We were trying to help.*

She nodded without answering and gazed at Eliza the spider. Eliza was scurrying along Mira's headboard, and when she reached the end she fell off and dangled by a silk thread.

"Oops," murmured Mira. "Let me give you a hand." She caught the thread and lifted it back up, but Eliza raced up in alarm and Mira jerked her hand back – straight into the web! It shrivelled and tangled, and Eliza scurried away in fear.

"Oh, *no*," Mira whispered, staring at the knotted mess. "Eliza, I'm so sorry! Oh, I've ruined it! I've ruined *everything*!"

Mira, it's not your fault— tried Flameteller again. But Mira shook her head and broke the connection, and Flameteller's voice disappeared. She put out the lamp and lay in her bed, staring up into darkness.

Things will seem better in the morning, Kai had told her, but when Mira awoke, it was still dark.

At first she thought it was still night, but then she remembered – the globes weren't working, and without them the cave would stay dark.

Erin and Cara weren't in the dorm. Mira lay in bed, wanting to stay there forever. But at last she sighed, lit her lamp and got dressed. When she left, she saw flickering lanterns here and there, and a glow coming from their dining hut. Mira wasn't hungry and couldn't face the others. She crept away.

DRAGON STORM

Against the wall of the cavern, a shimmering picture of the city glowed. Creedy and Nightwatcher stood by their scrying glass, concentrating on the image. Outside, it was daylight. Most of the citizens were going about their work, but a crowd had gathered and was moving through the town. Prince Harald was leading them – she could see his flowing blond hair even from here – and they stopped at each building to search. It wouldn't be long before they reached the entrance to the Guild. And with the Clockwork Corridors stuck wide open, they'd find it immediately.

Ahead of her she heard hammering, and saw more lamps. Daisy and Drun were building a barricade across the main doorway.

What would happen? Surely they could just talk to Prince Harald and find a way to prove they were friendly? Surely Berin could convince everyone they could trust the dragons! But she remembered Flameteller's words.

The humans are scared of us, he'd said. *Scared humans do strange things.*

She opened the path in her mind to let Flameteller through and he appeared immediately, dipping his head on to her shoulder.

"Oh, Mira," he said. "I was so worried about you!"

Mira gulped. "I'm sorry for cutting you off. You're not angry, are you?"

The dragon laughed softly and his warm breath surrounded her. "Of course not. You're my human."

Mira leaned against him and felt a little better. After a moment, she realised someone was coming towards her. It was Hilda, carrying a basket.

"Good morning, Mira, Flameteller," said Hilda cheerfully. "How are you today?"

Mira couldn't think how to answer that *at all*.

Hilda smiled. "Here." She reached into her basket and brought out a small pasty with a thick golden crust. "I'm bringing food round for the workers. Take one yourself."

Mira's stomach rumbled, but she hesitated. "Not me," she whispered. "I'm not a worker."

"Course you are," said Hilda. "You were working all day yesterday, and there's lots to do today."

"I don't … I don't think I deserve it," she murmured.

"Dearie me." Hilda nodded. "Let me tell you two things, my darling. First, *everyone* deserves a nice pasty now and then, and I won't have you turning one down."

Mira smiled shyly.

Hilda's pasties were famous and this one was still warm, steam rising in the cold cavern air.

"And second," said Hilda, "this is my own special recipe. It took me seventeen goes to get it right. You got to get the right filling, and the right consistency, and the right kind of pastry, and you got to cook it just right, and season it, and, oh, any amount of other things. Sixteen times I got it wrong. One time I set the oven on fire! Adults mess up just as often as children, let me tell you. And we're not so good at learning. So you take this, and you eat it and build your strength up. And if you broke something, figure out how to fix it, or how to help.

Mira and Flameteller

"But don't – and this is important, child, so listen – don't, *ever* –" she grinned – "turn down one of Hilda Brugarden's famous pasties again."

Despite herself, Mira laughed. "Sorry," she said, and took it. It smelled delicious.

"There," said Hilda. "Much better. Now, find yourself a space, eat up, and when you're ready, come and join us. It'll be fine."

"Thank you," said Mira. Hilda nodded, picked up her basket and headed away.

Mira still didn't feel she could face the others in the hut, so she headed back to her dorm and ate the pasty there. It was fantastic, hot and spicy, and despite her worries she felt better. Flameteller sat on the floor next to her bed. Dragons didn't need to eat in this world, but he liked the smell.

"What am I going to do?" she asked, sighing. The dragon shrugged.

"What *can* we do?" he asked. "What happened with the Dragon's Heart?"

"I wish I knew," said Mira.

"I could hear it," said Flameteller. "It was like it was trying to tell me something. All of it, the wheel, the mechanism…" He slapped a paw on the floor in frustration, raising a cloud of dust, and then sneezed. For a moment he looked so silly that Mira laughed.

"Hey," he said, looking past her. "Look at Eliza."

Mira turned and saw the little spider's web by her bed. Eliza had been busy overnight. The torn patch of web was still there, but she'd spun new silk round it, making wider circles and repairing most of the damage. The web wasn't perfect, but it was good again.

"Oh, thank goodness," said Mira. "I

thought I'd ruined your web as well as everything else!"

"All she needed was a bit of time to recover," said Flameteller.

Mira nodded. Then she stopped. "Oh," she murmured. "That's it. That's *it*."

Her heart sang. "That's it, Flameteller! I know what's wrong! Come on!" She stuffed the last of the pasty into her mouth, grabbed her lamp and raced for the door. "Hurry!"

"What? What is it? Where are we going?"

"We'll need help!" shouted Mira. "Come on! Oh, we can fix it – we can *fix* it!"

OLD NEW
WAYS

Mira raced towards the dining hut and reached it just as the others were leaving. They were quiet, and when they saw her they looked wary.

"We let you lie in," said Erin. "We thought you needed your rest."

Connor rolled his eyes. "Yes, after what you achieved yesterday."

Mira ignored him. "Everyone, I need your help," she said.

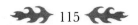

They stared at her.

"That's it?" asked Connor. "Not even, *I'm sorry?*"

Mira sighed. "Connor, I'm sorry. I was trying to help and there was an accident. It wasn't my fault but it happened because I was there, so I'm sorry. But I know *why* it happened! And I know what we have to do!"

They looked at each other. "OK," said Tom at last. "Why did it happen?"

"It was Flameteller who made me realise," said Mira. "And the dust. There *is* something wrong with the Dragon's Heart. Flameteller says it *sounds* wrong. And it's too hot, and swollen, and it's been stop-starting, and sometimes it's out of control…" Mira took a deep breath. "I think it's *sick*."

"What?" Connor frowned. "Mira, it's a thing, not an animal. I mean, I know it's magic, but it can't get *sick*."

"How do you know?" asked Mira.

Connor glanced at Kai. "What do you think?"

Kai was interested in medicine. He looked thoughtful. "It does sound like an infection. But the explosion?"

"I think that was a *sneeze*," said Mira.

"Huh," said Kai. "Maybe. It might have been a convulsion – that happens sometimes if you get a fever." He nodded. "It's possible."

Connor raised his hands. "Even if that's true, how do we cure a magic item?"

"I've no idea," said Mira. "But maybe we don't need to. It's over a thousand years old; it must be pretty good at looking after itself. Maybe we just need to give it time to recover."

"We don't have time," said Cara. "Prince Harald's men are getting close and we can't

move the Corridors."

"We tried this morning," said Tom. "Even the dragons can't turn the machinery."

"But maybe we can find something else," said Mira. "An alternative power source, just enough so we can let the Heart recover. I've got an idea, but I'll need your help."

She told them what she had in mind.

Connor scratched his chin. "Doubtful."

"It will work," said Mira. "*Trust me.* Come on – the adults are all busy. We're sitting just waiting, but we could fix things!"

The others hesitated, and Mira's heart sank. But then Erin sighed.

"Mira," she said. "You're exhausting, and you talk too much, and you break things *a lot.* But you've always got interesting ideas, I'll give you that. All right then – count me in!"

Tom grinned. "Me too." Even Connor sighed and nodded.

"Right," said Mira. "Let's go and save the Guild."

The young dragonseers and their dragons crept through the storeroom and down to the dock.

Grimbal wasn't there. Mira wondered if he was trying to get the Clockwork Corridors working. Tom lifted his lamp and whistled at the mess. The dock was almost destroyed, and the workshop floor was underwater.

Mira and Flameteller

Barrels and ropes floated or lay scattered like wreckage on a beach. The canal roared with white water, but everything else was quiet – no moving machinery, no ticking from the Dragon's Heart.

"This way," whispered Mira.

The Heart's cover was still open and it throbbed with an unsteady, slightly yellow light. The wheel around it moved and stopped, moved and stopped, like the hand of a clock that had nearly wound down, which was trying to turn but was too weak. Mira put out her hand and patted the covering. She didn't dare touch the Heart itself.

Connor peered through the hole in the

engine room, and at the river wall.

"That was some sneeze," he said.

"Prince Harald's moving again," called Ellis from outside the room. Ellis had positioned himself on a dry spot in the docks, listening for Cara. Cara was at the top, listening for her dragon, Silverthief – and Silverthief, who could stay hidden and even invisible, was up in the Guild Hall, watching the scrying image on the wall. Together they formed a human/dragon chain, sending down reports.

"He's close!" called Ellis. "He's reached our part of town."

"So what do we do?" asked Erin.

Mira looked at Flameteller. "What do you

think?" she asked.

"I can hear the mechanism," the dragon muttered. "It *wants* to move. If we can connect everything up, it might work—"

"Grimbal's coming!" called Ellis suddenly, behind them.

"Hide!" shouted Mira.

But it was too late – he was already stomping through the workshop. "What're you lot doing here?" he demanded. "Get back to the surface!"

He entered the engine room and glared at Mira and Flameteller. *"You two!"* He gasped. "Ain't you done enough damage?"

Mira raised her hands. "Grimbal, I'm trying to help—"

"Like last time? Look what you did!"

Mira nodded. "I know, but I've got an idea—"

"You don't know what you're doing!" he shouted. "You ain't got a clue!"

"Well, neither do *you*!" she snapped.

Grimbal blinked. "How dare you—" he started, but Mira kept going.

"You *knew* the Dragon's Heart was sick, didn't you?" she demanded. "You knew, and you didn't know how to fix it!"

"Well, I—"

"All that stuff you said to Berin about ideas you had – that was all made up! Admit it – you don't know what to do!"

Grimbal glared at her and pulled himself

up to
his full
h e i g h t
with a
f u r i o u s
expression.
"Young lady,"
he started.
"I... I..."

And then he stopped.

His shoulders slumped and
he seemed to deflate, and the angry
crease on his forehead lifted into one of
helplessness. He collapsed into a chair and
sagged.

"It's been happening for months," he

moaned. "Just a bit, at first. I think… I think she's *dying*."

Mira gaped at him. "Why didn't you *tell* someone?"

"You don't know what it's like!" he protested. "They're all depending on me, like I know how to fix everything!" His head sank. "But I don't. I don't know what to do."

The children stared at each other. Hesitantly, Mira patted his shoulder. "It's OK," she said. "I have a plan. We just need a source of power."

"But we don't have one!" wailed Grimbal.

"Well, actually we do…" Mira turned and pointed through the hole in the wall, to the raging river behind them. She grinned.

"We can build a *waterwheel*."

For a moment Grimbal's face lifted, but then he shook his head.

"Don't be daft, child. There's no waterwheel in the world as strong as the Heart!"

"But we don't need that much power," said Mira. "All we need is enough to move the Corridors for now. Just enough to give the Dragon's Heart time to recover. I think it *can* recover."

She looked at Grimbal. "I don't know if I'm right. And I don't know how to build a waterwheel. I'll need your help. But we can *try,* can't we?"

Grimbal scowled and chewed his lip,

gazing at the Dragon's Heart and its weak light. Then he nodded and stood. "All right," he said. "We can try."

"Prince Harald's only two streets away!" shouted Ellis.

Mira lifted her chin. "Let's get started."

FLAME
TELLER

Grimbal and Mira gave the orders and the children got to work, and their dragons too – Tom's mighty friend Ironskin, Connor's clever, wily Lightspirit, and Kai's solid Boneshadow. Erin couldn't summon Rockhammer by herself, so she settled for shouting orders at everyone else's dragons and insisting on carrying the heaviest of everything.

"We'll need an axle," said Mira. "And

somewhere to hold it on the other side."

"There are mooring pins on the river wall," said Grimbal, pointing. "There and there. But they won't hold for long."

"We only need a little bit," said Mira.

"We could use the main shaft from the Heart," muttered Grimbal, scribbling calculations down with a pencil. "It's long enough, I reckon…"

"And we'll need blades for the wheel."

"And something to build a wheel out of."

"What type should we go for?" he asked. "Overshot, backshot?"

Mira thought. "Backshot, if we can," she said thoughtfully. "More efficient and less—"

"Less turbulence," he finished, and

nodded. "Good thinking, lass." Mira beamed. Grimbal turned to the others. "Right, you lot!" he shouted. "We need flat pieces of wood, and poles to make wheel spokes out of! Anything you can, chop-chop!"

They raced over the workshop and docks, looking for anything they could use.

"What about doors?" asked Connor. "We could break the doors into parts."

"Good thinking!" shouted Mira.

"I've found the remains of the barge!" called Erin. "It's all smashed up but there are lots of flat pieces!"

"Bring them all here!" called Mira. She chewed her lip. "We don't have much time."

They hammered and sawed, tied and fastened, and Cara and Ellis sent them reports from upstairs. The adults were forming lines of defence. Prince Harald's mob was only a street away. They had to hurry. They had to *hurry*. It was a terribly rushed job. Would it work?

"Ready!" called Mira. "Ironskin, give us a hand!"

The huge dragon leaned down and heaved the wheel up on to its edge.

"It looks pretty rough," said Connor doubtfully.

Mira nodded. "It'll have to do. We'll roll it across now. Ready?"

"Wait!" said Flameteller suddenly. "One

of the spokes is loose – I can hear it!"

They found the piece and tightened it.

The dragon nodded. "It wants to work, but it's fragile."

"Come on!" called Grimbal.

Together, they rolled the wheel to the edge of the canal. The dragons lifted it into the air, beating their wings hard, and carried it over the water.

"OK, very slowly, lower!" ordered Mira. She was worried. Once the wheel was moving, it would be OK, but when it first touched the raging current… They lowered it, but then Flameteller roared.

"Back up!" They lifted it again. Flameteller said, "The river's too fast! The wheel can't hold; it's too weak. It's *scared*."

Mira gazed at him. "You can really *hear* that?"

Flameteller looked surprised. "Yes," he said. "Can't you?"

"No," said Mira. "No one can. Flame … I think this might be your *power*. You can hear machinery…" She stopped. "Can you *talk* to it?"

The dragon tipped his head to one side. "I'm not sure… Perhaps?"

"Try!" said Mira. "Talk to it! Persuade it to hold together or something – just until it starts spinning!"

Flameteller gazed at her. His wings beat in the air – those curious wings, with their

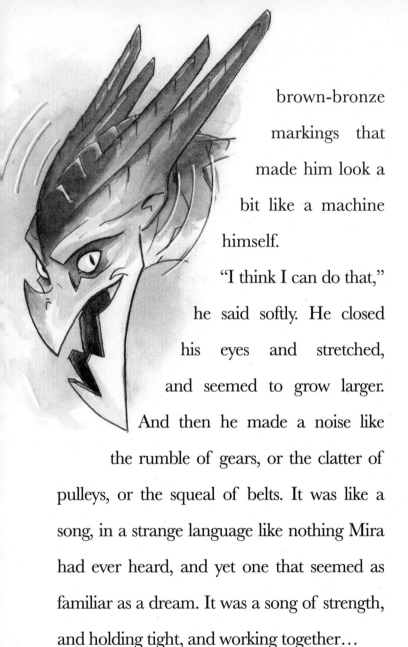

brown-bronze markings that made him look a bit like a machine himself.

"I think I can do that," he said softly. He closed his eyes and stretched, and seemed to grow larger. And then he made a noise like the rumble of gears, or the clatter of pulleys, or the squeal of belts. It was like a song, in a strange language like nothing Mira had ever heard, and yet one that seemed as familiar as a dream. It was a song of strength, and holding tight, and working together…

Mira and Flameteller

"Now," he murmured. The dragons lowered the spindle into the water and the wheel spun furiously. The wooden slats and spokes creaked and rattled, but held. And all the time Flameteller sang to the wheel, encouraging it, telling it how well it was doing, keeping it together...

"It's in place!" roared Grimbal. "Get the belt!"

The children lined up the belt that would connect the wheel shaft to the Clockwork Corridors.

"Ready?" called Mira. "Contact!"

There was a shriek of gears, and a squeal as the belt attached to the spinning shaft. Would it hold? Flameteller sang to it again as it skidded and squealed, until, until …

… until it gripped and started turning with the shaft. And above them, the great mechanism started shifting, and the pulleys moved and ropes whipped past and wheels spun.

Mira and Flameteller

"They're on the street!" called Ellis. "Prince Harald is on the street! They're only two houses away!"

"Will it work?" asked Mira.

Grimbal stared at the workings. "It's going to be close…" he whispered.

"They're at the cottage!" shouted Ellis.

And then, far away, they heard a *clunk*. Then a noise like a huge mechanical giant turning over in its sleep, and a whirr, and Grimbal smiled and closed his eyes.

"That was it," he murmured. "That was it. The passage is closed."

Mira let her head sink in relief. She felt as if she could sleep for a week.

"They've moved on to the next house,"

called Ellis. "They've moved on!"

All around Mira the machinery hummed and danced and clattered and roared and found its rhythm, and in front of her Flameteller sang along.

"You did it," she whispered.

"*We* did it," he murmured, and continued with his song. And behind them, the Dragon's Heart grew dim, and its cover closed, and it went to sleep.

NEW OLD
WAYS

It was a special occasion, so Grimbal was wearing his best brown coat. Mira grinned when she saw him.

"Looking sharp, Mr G," she said, and he nodded.

"Thank you. Are we ready?"

"They're coming down now."

He nodded again. He seemed a little distracted.

It was a few weeks later, and the workshop

and dock were almost restored. The canal was still raging, and the hole in the river wall still gaped, but the flood defences had held. And…

"Have you been tidying?" Mira asked.

"Well, you know, just here and there," Grimbal mumbled. He seemed a little embarrassed.

Mira smiled. "Looks good. Here they come now."

A procession came down the stairs, lamps bobbing as they walked. Chancellor Berin first, and then Vice Chancellor Creedy, and then Hilda, Drun and Daisy, and the children. They entered the engine room.

"Good afternoon, Mr Grimbal," said

Berin.

Grimbal bowed. "Yer Ladyship."

"Are we all ready?"

Grimbal and Mira glanced at Flameteller, and he nodded. Berin smiled.

"Very well," she said. "Begin."

Grimbal walked over to the wall where the Dragon's Heart sat under its brass cover, in the centre of the frozen wheel. He opened the panel and lifted the spanner. Hesitating, he turned to Mira.

"Here, lass," he said, offering it. "You do it."

Mira gulped. Carefully, she turned the dial to open the cover, just a line at first, then two halves, pulling apart … and there was the

Dragon's Heart. It pulsed slowly, with only a faint light. But the light was clean and pure now, and there was no stain.

"She's feeling much better," said Grimbal happily. "She went to sleep once we disconnected. Just needed a bit of time to recover."

Berin smiled. "I'm very pleased to hear that." She stepped forward and touched the tip of her staff against the diamond. The tip glowed blue, and the Dragon's Heart glowed back clear and strong, brighter and brighter. Around it, the wheel started moving in a steady tick, and the shaft behind it turned, and cogs whirred…

And above them, the globe lights lit up

with their calm, soft glow.

Erin started cheering, and the adults clapped. Even Vice Chancellor Creedy gave a pale smile. Berin turned to Mira, Flameteller and Grimbal, and bowed.

"Well done," she said.

Mira blushed.

"And the waterwheel?" asked Berin.

Mira nodded. "Now the Heart's better, we can disconnect the wheel. And then we can repair the wall and get the canal back to normal."

"And will the Heart be all right from now on?"

"Should be," said Grimbal. "Course, I don't know everything. Still a few tricks I

could learn, I reckon." He winked at Mira.
"But if the old girl needs a rest, we can put
the waterwheel back for a bit, now and then."

"It's always good to have an alternative,"
said Berin, smiling.

Later, Berin sat in her office with Mira and
Flameteller.

"Grimbal suggested you run the project to
repair the river wall," she said.

Mira grinned. "I'd love to!" she said. "I
was thinking we can put in a sluice gate and
an adaptable wheel. Then, when we need
to, we can increase the water pressure and
generate additional power, and then—"

Berin lifted a hand. "I'm sure you'll do a

good job," she said, smiling. She nodded to Flameteller. "And congratulations on your new power!"

The dragon purred with happiness. "Thank you."

"A dragon who can hear the songs of machinery," mused Berin. "A dragon who can *sing* to machinery…" Her cheeks creased. "Drun is very excited about that. He says he doesn't know how to classify you. He thinks you might be something never seen before." She nodded. "Perhaps you're *both* something new."

She stood and walked to the window of her office.

"This is the Dragonseer Guild," she said. "Here for over a thousand years. And although we are new to it, we are all trying to learn from the old ways."

She smiled at Mira. "But not *just* the old ways. We must learn some new ways of our own, even us ancient ones. What did Grimbal say? Still a few tricks we could learn? We try to teach you young dragonseers what we know. But perhaps … we need you to teach us what *you* know too?"

"Perhaps we should run a class," Mira said with a grin.

Berin laughed. "Perhaps! Thank you, Mira. That will be all."

Mira hesitated. "Miss?"

"Hmm?"

"What's going to happen outside?"

Berin sighed. "The mob died down when Prince Harald found nothing. But King Godfic knows we're here somewhere. He believes we have stolen something from his chambers. He is scared, and scared humans do strange things. And there are other mysteries – the other dragon Tom saw near the palace, the fact that the king even *had* a

Dragon's Eye... Something is going on and we must all be on our guard."

Mira nodded.

Berin smiled. "But that's a problem for another day. Go! Take today off and report to Grimbal tomorrow for your new project."

Mira bowed. "Yes, miss."

She walked back to the dormitory with Flameteller.

"That was nice," he said, stretching his neck for her to scratch.

Mira smiled. "Yes."

"So what shall we do now?" asked the dragon. "Take today off?"

"Sure," said Mira. "Or... Maybe we could visit the engine room, just for a little bit. There might be something that needs fixing."

"Good idea," said Flameteller. They entered the storeroom and wandered down to the docks, and the workshop. And Flameteller sang his song to the machines, and the machines sang back.

Look out for more books in
the Dragon Storm series:

KAI AND BONESHADOW
ERIN AND ROCKHAMMER